The Law of
Attraction

The Law of Attraction

WRITTEN BY

SHEILA SAVANNAH JOHNSON

AND TAMARA DERRICOTTE RIOS

Palmetto Publishing Group, LLC
Charleston, SC

The Law of Attraction
Copyright © 2017 by Sheila Savannah Johnson and Tamara
Derricotte Rios

For more information regarding special discounts for bulk
purchases, please contact Palmetto Publishing Group at
Info@PalmettoPublishingGroup.com.

ISBN-13: 978-1-944313-56-2
ISBN-10: 1-944313-56-7

THIS STORY IS ABOUT THE LOVE OF MY LIFE. I wasn't expecting it. I guess that's how real love works. It comes unexpectedly.

It was Monday morning, and I was staring at my computer at work. I'm an investigative reporter for Channel 7 in Savannah, Georgia. This day started like every other Monday. As I turned on my computer, my scheduler came up: 10 a.m. Call Carlton Monroe, Esq.

"Yes!" I said to myself. "I will get this interview!" I'd been trying to reach him for weeks to no avail. "I guess he thinks he's all that now, since he won that big case against the tobacco company." Determined, I picked up the phone, and called his office again. I had dialed this number so much that the number had saved on my call log.

"Monroe Law Firm, Carlton Monroe speaking."

His voice startled me, because I was expecting to hear his Gatekeeper answer—I mean, *receptionist*.

"Hi, Mr. Monroe," I said, slightly startled. "My name is Candice Lee from Channel 7, here in Savannah."

"Oh hi, Ms. Lee. I'm very sorry I haven't got back

to you."

"No problem. But I have to tell you, I was starting to take it a little personally."

"Oh, no. Never," Carlton said. "I Just finished up a big trial, and I just happened to come back to my office."

"Well, I guess this is my lucky day," I said, giggling flirtatiously.

"Well, what can I do for you, ma'am?" he asked.

"I would like to have an interview with you about how you single handedly took down the Rengal Tobacco company. It's a real David-and-Goliath story, and you have become a local hero."

"I was planning to have a press conference on Wednesday." He paused, and said, "But I like you. I've seen your stories on the news before, and you really seem to care about the community. I'll tell you what— I'll meet with you and give you an exclusive. Since I feel bad about not getting back to you after all those messages that you left."

A slight smile came over my face, and I responded in a calm voice, "Great! How does 10 a.m. tomorrow sound?"

"Ten, tomorrow," he said, and paused. "Ten sounds good. I'll see you then."

I hung the phone up, and I screamed in my office. Yes! I swung around in my chair, raised my hands up to God, and gave thanks! I knew it was going to be a career-changing interview.

∽

As I drove home, I kept thinking about my interview. *I can't wait to tell John,* I thought to myself. My husband, John "Two Punch" Lee, is a Local legend, and a successful businessman—a Gold-medal winner in the 2008 Olympics. He received many big-name endorsements. With that success, he was able to turn his brand into a successful chain of boxing gyms along the East Coast, including our home base in Savannah, where he trains fighters. He even has a street named after him: John "Two Punch" Lee Boulevard. He owns the city—and me. Our marriage, from the outside, is like a fairy tale: two beautiful people, each of us successful in our own right; an exquisite, seven-bedroom home on the lake; our twin sons, Jacob and Dak, who attend North Carolina A&T. Jacob is the starting, wide receiver, and already has NFL scouts looking at him. Dak is a member of North Carolina A&T Marching Band, and is on the famous drumline, which is world renowned. We are the epitome of a power couple, but that's on the outside. Inside is a different story. You see, John has many followers—as you might imagine—and being faithful is not high on his list of priorities.

John is also master of manipulation when it comes to me. Once, when he came back from Thailand after he'd been there for a match, he gave me an STD! His explanation was simple—someone put gonorrhea in his underwear. John also has two children outside of our marriage he takes care of financially; otherwise, they are not in his life. Those explanations, to him, were just as simple. "I got drunk, and I didn't realize what happened," is what he told me. He knew that I would believe him, or at least accept his excuses as truth. John knew that I'd never received love from the first man in my life—my father—so he used that to his advantage. He knew all he had to say was that he loved me, and I would believe it. He also knew my commitment to my family wouldn't allow me to leave him. John knew the struggle that I went through as a child; my mother working hard to support the family as a nurse, all while dealing with a husband who was abusive toward us.

As I thought about sharing the good news with John, I remembered the argument we had just a few days ago. The twins' Homecoming was this weekend, and we were major donors to the University, so we go every year. But this year John told me he may not be going this weekend.

"How could you not go this year?" I'd said to him. "You know that Jacob has the scouts looking at him?"

I started to tear up a little as I relived the argument,

and then stopped myself. *I'm not going to let him rain on my parade. I'm not going to mention it. If he doesn't know anything about it, then he can't criticize it*, I thought to myself as I pulled into the garage.

∽

The next day, I was in a great mood. I knew I was about to do the interview of a lifetime. As I walked to my office I kept looking at my phone. Ten o'clock couldn't get here soon enough. After I met with my assistant and the cameraperson, we got in the van and drove to Mr. Monroe's office. I looked at my phone.

"Ten o'clock on the dot," I said to my team. "Now let's do this!"

They all got out of the van and went inside. Mr. Monroe was waiting for them in the lobby.

"Good morning, everyone," Mr. Monroe said. "Welcome, and have a seat."

"Is this okay to set up out here?" I asked.

"Sure," Mr. Monroe answered.

This is great, I thought to myself as I stuck my hand out to shake his. Now I knew Mr. Monroe was handsome from his photos and the ads I'd seen all around town, but I didn't know how charming he was. Mr. Monroe grabbed my hand, placing his on top of mine, and rubbing ever so gently. This startled me a little, because I hadn't expected him to put such a soft touch into a handshake.

Mr. Monroe was much taller than I expected, at least six foot two, and he had a slight accent. But it was his presence that stood out the most. Mr. Monroe exuded a masculinity about himself that couldn't be contained—or denied—and I found myself very much drawn to it. After I pulled myself together, I again thanked Mr. Monroe for allowing us to come in and do the exclusive interview on the trial.

Thirty minutes went by—and cut.

"Thank you so much, Mr. Monroe," I said. "That was great." I thanked him again, and Mr. Monroe escorted us to the door, shaking each member of my team's hands as they went out the door. When I turned to shake his hand again, he grabbed my hand with both of his hands, and told me how much he enjoyed my questions.

"I'm glad that they were acceptable to you," I said, feeling slightly flushed by his touch.

He then leaned down and kissed me on the cheek, smiled, and said "Please, call me 'Carlton.' And I want to thank you for being persistent."

As I walked out of the door, I could feel him staring at me. I turned to get into the van as he waved goodbye. Somehow, I knew it wouldn't be the last time we saw each other.

◇

After work, I came home to an empty house. I guessed that John was still at the gym. I made a cup of my favorite herb tea I'd picked up from Tiny's place. Tiny is one of my best friends who I grew up with. She owns a trendy cafe downtown on the Savannah River called Sweet Surrender.

It was raining outside, so I decided to take advantage of the peacefulness of my home without John's presence. Just then, the phone rang. It was TC, my oldest sister, who lives in Nigeria.

"I was just thinking about you!" I said to her.

"I know," TC answered. "I felt it all the way across the ocean." She laughed.

We are very close. TC is like a mother to me in many ways. She even helped me pick out the college I attended. TC is an educator who lost her husband a few years ago to cancer. They both had a dream to build a school in Nigeria, so TC moved there a year ago to complete the dream that she and her husband shared.

"How's the school coming?" I asked.

"Great! The donations that you put together allowed us to build a new swimming and tennis complex. And the children love it!"

"That's great..." I trailed off.

"What's wrong, sis?" TC asked. "I know you.

7

Something is going on."

"I'm just thinking about how Dad treated Mom and the rest of us," I said.

"Candice, you have to let go of those old memories. They are in the past. Those memories made you who you are today, but they don't make you who you are tomorrow. *You* control that. You make your destiny!"

I knew that TC was right, so I changed the tone of my voice. We talked a little more, and then we said our good byes.

༄

It was a beautiful day in Savannah, seventy-eight degrees, with a nice, cool breeze. I woke up excitedly, because it was my birthday. I looked over to see John still sleeping. *Well, I guess there's no breakfast in bed for me today,* I thought as I reached for my phone. Refusing to allow myself to get depressed, I jumped out of bed, and went to bathroom.

"I going to the office today," I said to John.

"Okay," he answered as he rolled over. *He didn't even remember it was my birthday,* I thought, turning on the shower. Just then, I heard my phone ring.

"Asia?" I said into the phone. "Hey! You're in town!"

"Of course," Asia said. "I'm getting my bags now."

Asia is the second part of the trio of friends I've

had since childhood. We sang in the children's choir at church, and we're all fraternity sisters. I was Asia's maid of honor at her wedding.

"How's the wine business?" I asked as I brushed my teeth.

"It's doing great!" Asia said. "I've got a case of Moscato we just finished up at the winery that's ready for your approval! I'll meet you at Tiny's."

"Well, I gotta go to the office first, and then I'll meet you over there," I said.

"Great!" Asia said. "I'll see you then."

I smiled to myself. Asia is one my best friends in the world—sister is more like it. Tiny, is the other. The three of us had been friends since middle school. Everyone used to call us "Destiny's Child" because we were together all the time. We were inseparable. Asia's husband, Sean Onornto, owns a winery in Italy and one in Napa Valley. Yes, the three friends did well for ourselves. *I'm thankful, God*, I thought as I finally got into the shower. I'm grateful for great friends and an amazing career, but with all of those blessings in my life, I still feel an emptiness that I can't ignore. *God, I just want to feel real love in my life.* A familiar sadness came over me as tears started to roll down my face. *God, why do I feel this hole deep inside my core?! My babies are grown now. It's time for me to fill this hole.*" I then thought about my dad, Luis. *I just wanted him to love me.* But he just showed me his hand—usually across my face.

It was hard for me to think of my Dad in a loving way. The things he did to me were cruel, and I feel his abrasive words haunting me from his grave even now. I don't blame him, though. I know that my father was a very cold individual. He lived in a time where it was hard to be a black man in America. I knew he loved me. He just didn't know how to show it. I was determined not to allow that generational curse to be placed on my children.

But what about myself? Now that my kids are older I know I have to address those demons that attack my subconscious. Am I even worthy of love—real love? *Do I have the right to complain? God, I know that I am deserving of love. I know that you have someone for me who will love me for who I am.* Tears started to fall down my face again. I got out of the shower, and patted my face with a towel. The shower is a great place to let tears go freely. I looked in the mirror, and then went to the closet to get dressed. John was still asleep in the bed.

"I'm going to the office," I said to John as I left the house.

⟡

When I got to work I saw a beautiful bouquet of flowers on my desk! *Awww, John remembered after all.* As I walked to the flowers, smiling, I bent down to smell the beautiful lilies and read the card. "Happy Birthday, Mom!" *Oh! My babies sent these. I love them,* I thought as I put the card back on the flowers. I was grateful to receive them, but a part of me felt disappointment that they weren't from John.

Meanwhile at Sweet Surrender, Asia pulled up to the cafe. She saw Tiny outside putting up the last umbrella on her tables

"Tiny!" Asia screamed.

"Hey, Asia!" Tiny screamed back, as Asia jumped out of the car. They hugged and went into the restaurant.

"Lisa!" Tiny called to her assistant. "Please bring us some glasses so I can test out this new vino."

"I'm glad you didn't sample it without me here," said Asia.

"No," Tiny said. "I promised I would wait until you got here this time."

As Asia opened the bottle of wine, she asked Tiny, "Is everything set for the surprise party tonight?"

"Yes," Tiny said. "Everything is set to go. Carl, Candice's assistant, called this morning and is bringing over the cake after work."

"Well, is John going to make it this time, or does he have another 'appointment' that he can't reschedule?" Asia asked sarcastically.

"Of course not!" Tiny said. "He has to train his

star fighter, 'Romi.' She's ranked number one in the world—but we'll kick her ass if she messes with our girl's husband!"

"Damn right!" Asia said. "I'm not gonna think about their shit no more. Only positive thoughts right now for our girl."

"Yes!" Tiny agreed as they toasted their glasses.

I walked through the door just then.

"What's up, ladies?!"

"Hey!" they screamed, and the three of us all hugged each other. We sat down, and they grabbed me a glass.

"A toast to the birthday girl! Happy birthday, sis!" They raised their glasses.

"Yeah, my own husband didn't even wish me a happy birthday," I said. I looked down as I started to tear up.

"No, ma'am! Don't you start that crying now. We got you—no matter what!"

"Don't worry, Candice," Tiny said. "You're coming back here for dinner tonight."

"I don't know what I would do without you guys," I said as I wiped a single tear that came down, even though I'd tried to stop it.

Asia then said, "Let's get something to eat. We're drinking already."

"Yes, we are," Tiny said. "Cause we're celebrating!

So let's get some lunch."

"Alice!" Tiny called. "We're ready to order."

Alice, the waitress came over. "What can I get for you ladies today?" she asked.

"I'll have the mushroom-Swiss-veggie on wheat. I just added this to the menu, and I want you both to try it," Tiny said.

"That sounds good for me," Asia said.

"Me too, "I chimed in.

Asia pulled out her e-cig. "I have exactly what we need to relax," she said. "Straight from the Emerald Triangle!"

"What's that, girl?" I asked, laughing. "You know I don't do that stuff!"

Asia laughed. "Girl! This is a perfect blend for what ails you. My doctor prescribed a special blend for you. I told him what was going on, and that I was going to be seeing you for your birthday."

We sat at our table passing it around and laughing.

"I can't," I said. "I gotta go back to finish up a few things at work, and then change clothes. I'll meet you guys back here at seven."

Just then, I heard someone come through the door. It was Carlton Monroe.

"Well hello, ladies," he said with a smile that could melt an iceberg! Shocked, I looked away.

"Oh, hi, I stuttered.

"Hey, Carlton," Tiny said. "You want your regular?"

"You know it, Tiny," Carlton said. He laughed. "You have the best food on the river. I'll take the house special. Hello, Candice," he said to me as he reached out his hand. "I didn't know you came here."

"Yes," I said. "This is my sister's restaurant."

"Oh," Tiny said. "You guys know each other?"

"Yes, this Hero brought down the big tobacco company," I said.

"Wow," Tiny said. "Congratulations, Carlton! I didn't know."

"Thank you," Carlton said. "And thank you, Candice, for that wonderful story you did. I appreciated how you presented me in that story."

"Well, I was just being honest," I said. "You are a hero in my book for bringing those guys down!" I leaned down to get my purse and stood up. "Well, I better be going ladies. I'll see y'all tonight."

As I pulled out my wallet to pay for the meal, Carlton said, "No, I have this, ladies. Lunch is on me today."

"Wow, that's very nice of you," Asia said.

I smiled as I put my wallet back in my purse. "It was very nice seeing you again, Mr. Monroe," I said as I extended my hand to shake his.

"Please, call me 'Carlton,'" he said as he grabbed my hand and kissed it. He then walked to the counter to pay for the meals. I smiled and turned to Asia and Tiny.

"Girl...that's a fine piece of chocolate there! And you know how I love chocolate," Asia whispered. "He was looking at you like you were a lollipop—wanting to lick you up and down!

"Stop it!" I whispered, and then the three of us busted out laughing.

"He's married, though," Tiny said. Just then, the song "Me and Mrs. Jones" started playing in the background. We all burst out laughing again, and sang along.

"Ya'll are crazy!" I said. "I'll see you ladies later."

Carlton, with his meal in hand, walked over to Tiny and Asia, and asked, "You guys have something happening tonight?"

"Yes," Tiny said. "We're having a surprise birthday dinner for Candice. Hey, why don't you come out tonight?"

"That sounds like fun," Carlton said. "What time?"

"Be here at six thirty. Candice should be here at 7."

"I'll be there," he said. "What can I bring as a gift? I really wanted to do something nice for her to thank her for that great story she did."

"Well, she likes the ocean," Tiny said.

"Okay, I'll keep that in mind." He smiled, and then walked out of the restaurant.

"Damn, girl! He really is fine," Asia said.

"That he is," said Tiny. "Did you see how he looked at Candice? He couldn't stop staring at her!"

"I know!" Asia said. "Did you see how Candice was blushing? They definitely have chemistry."

"I can't wait to see Candice's face tonight," said Tiny. She and Asia gave each other a high five.

"Yes, indeed. This is going to be *some* night tonight!" said Asia, and the two drank down the rest of their wine.

∽

When I pulled in the garage, John was getting in his car.

"Where you going?" I asked.

"Gotta work out Romi," John said. "You know the match is coming up."

"Yes," I said, as we passed each other. *Not even a happy birthday?*

"Oh yeah, happy birthday," he said. "We'll do something after the match."

"*No* problem," I said. *I've heard that before,* I thought as I started to tear up. *I'm* not *going to let him bring me down this birthday—not today!* I went into the house. When I went to the bedroom to hang up my clothes, I noticed a receipt on the floor. *What's this?* I thought, as I looked at it. Maybe John had surprised me by buying some sexy lingerie, but then I realized this wasn't for me.

"Size three?!" I yelled. "I don't wear no damn three!" Furious, I knew in my gut that the lingerie John had purchased was for Romi. I started to pace back and forth, tears running down my face. "I'm *not* going to cry! I'm not going to cry!" But the tears kept coming down. *I don't understand this, God! What did I do wrong? I'm faithful, I forgave him for all of his affairs, I'm trying to do the right thing...but I just can't take this!*

Right then, my phone rang. It was TC.

"Ku ojo ibi!" she said. "Happy birthday!"

"Thank You," I said, sobbing.

"What's wrong?!" asked TC. "Did John do something to you? That Bastard is cheating again!"

"I can't take this shit anymore!" I screamed. "*Why* do I stay in this marriage, TC? Why? Is it because of how Daddy treated us? I saw Mom stay through so many infidelities. I don't want to do this, but I can't leave!"

"Don't cry, baby sis. You'll know when you've had enough. I have your back...always," she said, trying to console me. "Don't cry."

"Thank you, TC. I love you, but I gotta go."

"Why? What are you going to do?" TC asked. "I don't want you to be there by yourself."

"I'll be okay," I said, wiping my tears. I should be use to this by now. I won't be by myself. Asia is in town, and we're meeting at Tiny's for dinner tonight."

"Good," TC said. "What are you going to do with John? Are you going to tell him what you know?"

"I don't know yet, but I'm not going to think about

SHEILA SAVANNAH JOHNSON & TAMARA DERRICOTTE RIOS

it anymore. I've cried enough tears about his ass today. And it's my birthday. I don't want to be sad on my birthday!"

"That's the right idea, sweetie. Don't think about it. Remember—call me if you need me. I'm here for you."

"Thanks, sis," I said, and hung up the phone. I put the receipt in my purse and went downstairs to get a shot of vodka. *I'm not going to let this ruin my birthday dinner,* I thought. *I will no longer be affected by his actions anymore!* I drank one shot...and then another. *I'm going to put on a beautiful dress, and have a great time with my friends. Happy Birthday to* me!

I went back upstairs to get dressed. After I took a long shower, I contemplated how I was going to confront John. Should I show him the receipt? Should I go to the gym? Feeling numb, I thought, *I will just forget it. It didn't happen...at least I'm going to treat it like that for today. I don't want anything to interfere with my night. I will have a great birthday! Damn, I wish I had that e-cig Asia brought right now!*

As I got dressed, I kept thinking about the receipt. "Fuck this! I'm going to the gym," I said as I looked at the receipt in my purse.

When I got to the gym, I saw John's car there.

"What's up, Candice?" Fran said to me as I walked in. Fran was John's Sister. She managed and did promotions for the gym.

"Hey, Fran. Where's John?"

"I'm not sure. I know he was just in the ring. He may be in the bathroom."

"Okay, thanks," I said as I walked toward the back of the gym to the locker room. When I walked in, I saw my husband sitting on the bench, Romi standing over him with her leg over his shoulder. She was naked from the waist down.

Shocked, I couldn't believe what I had just seen. I ran out of the gym, but no one even noticed. Fran called to me as I ran out, "What happen, Candie?"

I didn't answer. How could I answer Fran? What was I going to say? I got in my car, and just sat there in disbelief. *Did I just see what I thought I saw?* I thought. Crying, I tried to call Asia, but I couldn't even dial the numbers. *I should go in there and beat her ass!* But I was afraid that John would defend Romi. He would tell me that I hadn't seen what I just saw. He was very good at that—making me think that I was imagining things. I took a deep breath, and I decided I couldn't take that kind of rejection—not on my birthday. I lit a cigarette I found in my purse, and took a deep breath.

"I'll handle this," I said to myself. "But not today. Today, it's my birthday." I wiped my tears, checked myself in the rearview mirror, and drove to the restaurant.

∽

It was 6:30 p.m., and my assistant Carl was putting the last finishing touches on the decorations in the restaurant.

"Everything looks great, Carl," Tiny said. "I can't wait to see Candice's face when she walks in."

"Yes, everything looks beautiful," Asia said. "She's going to love it."

As my friends and other family members came in, Carl said to Tiny, "You know that a-hole of a husband knows about the party, and he said he couldn't make it."

"What?" Tiny asked. "I didn't know you invited him."

"Yes, mama. I did, and I knew he wasn't going to come. He gave me some damn excuse about having to train that biotch! I just don't understand why she won't divorce his ass! It's obvious that he has no love for her. I hate that she stays with him."

"Well," Tiny said, "I know that he loves her, but he just doesn't know how to show it. Not to mention, he's a workaholic."

"Well, I'm not going to speak about him anymore," Carl said. "This is about Candice tonight!"

Tiny was glad to switch the subject, because even though she agreed with Carl, she wasn't going to have him gossiping about her girl—or give him anything else to talk about.

I pulled up to the restaurant.

"Everyone, she's here!" Tiny exclaimed. "Take your places! Quick!"

Everyone then sat down at the tables that were lit with candles. No lights were on. I walked through the doors, and everyone yelled, "Surprise!"

The lights came on, and party favors sounded throughout the place.

"Oh my God!" I screamed. "I can't believe this!" Happy birthday came through the speakers. I was in tears, and I thanked everyone as I walked toward Tiny and Asia. "You guys were behind this, I know!" I said, laughing and wiping away tears.

"Of course—with Carl's help!"

"Yes, honey," Carl said. "You know I wasn't going to let this day go by without doing something special for you. You deserve it—and more! Now, everyone grab a glass, and let's do a toast."

As everyone raised their glasses, Carlton Monroe came through the door.

"Wait, wait! I gotta get in on this toast," he said, as he grabbed a glass from the bar and moved toward Candice.

"Wow! I didn't expect to see you here," I said, smiling.

"Yes, your posse told me about it, and I had to be here." He leaned in and gave me a kiss on the cheek.

"Happy birthday," he said.

"Okay, okay! Let's get this toast done, so we can start the party!" Carl said. As they held their glasses up, I smiled, feeling loved for the first time in a long time.

As the party went on, I went around thanking everyone for showing me so much love. No matter where I was in the room, I saw Carlton glancing at me, smiling that sexy smile.

"Damn, Asia," I said. "I keep catching his eye, no matter where I am in this room!" I giggled. "And the way I'm feeling right now, I may go up there and ask him why he keeps looking at me."

"You should, girl. He may have a gift for you—and not the kind in the box, if you know what I mean," said Asia.

I laughed, and said, "I wouldn't mind that at all!"

The music was playing, and everyone was dancing and having a great time. I sat at the table with Asia and Tiny, and suddenly I said, "I think I'm going to go up there. Asia, let me get a hit of that e-cig! I need it!"

Asia laughed as she pulled it out and gave it to me. Just as I finished puffing it, Carlton came up, and said, "How are you enjoying your surprise party?"

"I'm loving it," I answered. "Thanks so much for coming out!"

"I have a gift for you, but I wanted to give it to you in private," Carlton said. A laugh came from her girls at the table.

"I hear that," Asia said, hitting Tiny on her leg.

"Why don't you go in my office, Candi?" said Tiny. "You know where it is."

"Okay," I said, as I slid back to stand up. Carlton extended his hand again to help me up.

We headed back to Tiny's office. I was walking in front of him, and when I glanced back at him, I noticed how Carlton was watching me. I started to walk with a sway that hypnotized him like a metronome going back and forth.

I opened the office door, and we walked in. I leaned against the desk. Carlton pulled out a box and gave it to me.

"This is so nice. You really didn't have to buy me a gift."

"I wanted to show you my appreciation for doing such a great piece on me—and to also wish you a happy birthday," Carlton said. "I hope you like it."

I felt like a teenager, which surprised me. Feeling butterflies in my stomach, I opened the box. It was a beautiful necklace with an hourglass pendant that had sand and water inside of it.

"It's beautiful," I said. "I love this hourglass pendant. What's inside?"

"This is beach sand from St. Croix, and beautiful water from my ocean. I'm from St. Croix, and I have a jar with sand from our beautiful beaches and our crystal clear waters. I look at my jar whenever I get homesick. When I spoke with your friends today after you left, they said that you love the beach. So I thought, why not give you a little piece of something that you love so much? That way when you want to get away and can't, you can take a look at your pendant and have a piece of heaven right there in your hand. I know it helps me when I look at it—so I wanted to share it with you."

"Thank you so much. This is so thoughtful," I said. "I will keep it close to my heart."

"Let me put it on you," Carlton said.

I turned around, and lifted my hair so he could fasten the necklace. I turned back around.

"I love it!" I said as I gave him a hug. As we finished embracing, Carlton held me, looking into my eyes.

"You are such a beautiful woman...but your eyes are so sad," Carlton said, as he kissed me on the forehead.

A tear fell down my cheek as I said, "I've been sad for a very long time."

"No longer," he whispered to me. He picked me up in his arms, and gently placed me on the desk.

I put my hands up hesitantly. *What am I doing?* I thought to myself. I knew I shouldn't be doing this, but everything in my soul kept telling me to keep going. Carlton gently slid my legs open, and kissed me on my inner thigh. I arched my back, fearful, but I could not deny what he was doing to me. Dripping wet, I looked at him.

"Guide me," Carlton said.

I then grabbed his bald head, and guided him down. Carlton then opened me and placed his mouth on my most personal treasure. I felt a waterfall of passion come down as he blew on my womanhood so gently. He then he started to lick me like he was eating a juicy peach. Dripping everywhere, he then took me to a place that I've never been. I shook with ecstasy, not wanting to be heard outside these walls.

Carlton cradled me like a baby, rocking me back and forth. He then sat on the chair, positioning me, on top of him, pulling me up and down on his large cock.

"Oh my God," I screamed with pleasure, not caring if anyone heard me.

Carlton kept thrusting me up and down, until we both climaxed. Soaking wet, we trembled in each other's arms. Our bond seemed like it had been created in another time; two souls

finding their way back to each other. I placed my head on his chest, wanting this moment to freeze in time.

"What are we doing?" I asked, looking into Carlton's eyes.

"I don't know," he answered. "But I don't want this to end. I want you."

Back at the party, Asia and Tiny were wondering where the birthday girl was.

"Damn, Asia," Tiny said. "Candice and Carlton are still in the office?"

"I think so," Asia said.

"We better get her out of there before she does something she might regret—or not!"

They both laughed, as they walked back to the office. Just as they were about to knock on the door, Carlton and Candice came out.

"Wow! We were worried about ya'll," Asia said.

"Don't worry, ladies," Carlton said. "I have taken good care of your sister."

I laughed, and said, "Look at my gift. Isn't it beautiful?"

"Wow! It's gorgeous. What is it?" asked Asia.

"It's sand and water from St. Croix," I said, holding it up for them to see.

"Great gift," Tiny said, as she smiled at Carlton.

As we walked back to the party, guests were leaving. People said bye to me, and hugged me before they walked out. It seemed like a great time had been had by all.

∽

As I drove home, dazed, I thought, *What did I just do?* I

went into the house, and saw that John was fast asleep.

I went to take a shower. The warm water dripping down my body made me think of Carlton's hands on me. I started to think about Carlton as I rubbed soap over my body. My body moved with the rhythm of the memory we had just shared. Moving up and down with the water pouring against my body from the shower head, I withered in ecstasy, careful not to scream. I opened my eyes to see my reflection in the bathroom mirror. For the first time I saw myself—or the lack thereof.

Why am I allowing myself to not to be loved? I thought to myself as I got into bed. Tears began to fall down my face.

God, I know that you put love above all else, I prayed. *We are supposed to give and receive love. I appreciate the life that you've blessed me with—*my career, my children—*but I don't have love from my own husband. I don't understand that! My father didn't love me, and my husband doesn't love me either.*

Just then, my mind went to Carlton, and the passionate exchange we'd had at the party. *Carlton touched a place in me that I forgot existed—a passion so great, that I have been transformed. I'm not sure how to see myself anymore,"* I thought to myself. *I thought that I would never be able to have someone fill that vast canyon that remains when I'm not in his arms. Is it my fault for growing into the person that I have become? To have empathy for others who love completely has created a deeper longing for that same love in return. How was this man able to connect so completely with my soul?*

The tears continued down my face. Carlton had caused me to release emotion on a level that had escaped me—a level of love that I hadn't believed really existed. To experience this type of love for the first time in my life had really showed me what love should be. Without this release of emotion, love, for me, had been incomplete.

As I lay in my bed, I felt grateful. I knew that I had just experienced complete love—but what was I to do now? How could I go back to living without it?

❦

The next day at work, I couldn't concentrate. *Why is this guy calling me?* I thought, as I looked down at Carlton's number on my phone. I didn't dare answer for fear of what he might say. I was embarrassed, but intrigued at the same time—embarrassed, because I shouldn't have lost control. I'd never been unfaithful in my marriage before. But I couldn't deny the attraction I felt toward Carlton, as I imagined his hand gently caressing my breast. A shiver of ecstasy passed through my body.

"Damn," I said to myself. "I have to get away."

I called Asia, and asked if I could come out for a few days.

"Come on, girl," Asia said. "You know you're more than welcome. It would be great to see you again, and you can sample our new wine we're introducing."

"Great! I'll see you in a few days I guess." I heard a beep on the line. "Asia, I'll call you later. I have another call."

It was Carlton again. I sent the call to voicemail.

On my way home from work, I thought about the homecoming weekend at my son's university. *How am I going to go to A&T this weekend with John, knowing what I know?* I thought. *How would the boys feel if I didn't go with their father? How can I pretend that everything is okay after I saw him servicing that tramp Romi in the gym?! More importantly, though, how can I pretend after that night of passion I had with Carlton? I'm not like him. He will know. And I want to tell him what I saw, but not at the game. There's a right time for everything.*

"That's it. I can't go to the homecoming," I said to myself. The boys would understand. I called Asia, and told her I needed to come out there as soon as possible.

"Is everything okay there, sweetie?" Asia asked. "I know you. Isn't homecoming this weekend?

"Yes," I answered, "but I'm not going. The boys already know, and I really have to get out of here—or I'm going to go crazy! I've got some vacation days, and I've put in for them anyway because we were going to Greensboro for the boys' game—but I just can't go there with him."

"I understand, sweetie," Asia said. "You know you can come here, and you don't have to speak to anyone—only if you feel up to it."

"I'll look for a ticket tonight, and get back with you. Thanks so much, Asia," I said. "I really need to figure out what I'm going to do with my life."

Just then, I got another text from Carton. This time, I decided to respond. "Carlton, I can't see you. I'm going to Asia's for a few days. I have to clear my mind," I texted.

As I drove home, I kept thinking about John and how I would break it to him that I wasn't going to homecoming. When I pulled into the garage, I saw that John's car was gone.

"Where is this bastard? He's not home from work yet?!" I said to myself. When I walked into the house, I saw a note from John.

Candice, I had to go to the training hub for the weekend. Will see you in a week. John. P.S. I spoke with Franny, and she said she would go to Greensboro with you for the weekend.

Wow, I thought. *He didn't even have the decency to call—just leave a note.* Fed up, I threw a few clothes in a suitcase. I then wrote on the same note at the bottom:

No problem, John. I went to Asia's for the weekend. Will see you when I get back.

I called Fran, and told her that she could bring someone with her to the game. We had season tickets. I told her I would not be going.

"What happened, Candi?" Fran asked. "Why aren't you going to the game?"

"I just have to go to Asia's this weekend. I've already spoken with the boys, and they know we're not coming. They actually sounded happy."

"They probably are," Fran said. "These kids want to have a great time without their parents being there."

"I think you're right. But you can still go, and enjoy the festivities. John's not going—as you well know," I said.

"Yes, but I'm not sure why you're not going."

"I know. I just have a lot of thinking to do, and I need to be in a different place to think."

"I understand," Fran said. "I'll hold it down for the family."

"Thank you, Fran. I appreciate you so much."

Just then, I got a call from Asia.

"Hey, girl! I found a great deal on a ticket, but you have to leave tomorrow out of Atlanta. I've booked the ticket, so you have to go."

"Thank you, Asia," I said, tearing up. I can leave

tonight, and stay at a hotel."

"It's already done. I booked you a room at the Hilton Airport. Your plane leaves at eleven on Saturday."

"Wow. You thought of everything," I said.

"Yes, I did," Asia said. "So all you have to do is drive to Atlanta tonight and check in. I love you, and I'll see you tomorrow."

"Thank you, again, Asia. I don't know what to say."

"You don't have to say anything," Asia said. "Drive safe, and I'll see you tomorrow."

∽

Later, when I was driving, I started to tear up, but suddenly my thoughts went to Carlton. I started to smile, and I wiped my face. With the wind blowing in my hair, I started to feel a sense of freedom that I couldn't explain—but I welcomed it. A peaceful feeling came over me, and I turned up the music.

∽

It was a beautiful day in Napa, and as I woke up, Asia came through the door of the guest room.

"Good morning, sunshine," she said. She was carrying two cups of coffee. "Time to rise and shine and enjoy life!"

"Thanks so much, sis, for letting me come for the weekend," I said, as I took one of the cups. Asia asked why I needed to get away.

"I just can't take living in a loveless marriage any longer," I said to her. "I just need to sort out what I should do. I walked in on John performing oral on that bitch, Romi.

"Whaaaat?!?!" Asia yelled. "When?"

"It's okay, though, because I fucked Carlton in Tiny's office!"

"What?!" Asia screamed, and started jumping up and down.

I jumped up, and slapped high-five with Asia.

"It was crazy how it came about! It was like karma just said, 'Here, I'm gonna give you one—just because it's your birthday!'" I laughed. Those laughs turned into tears, though, and I started to cry. "I thought I didn't deserve to have someone love me," I said. "My daddy didn't show me love, so I didn't think I would ever feel that. I became numb. So when I saw them in the gym, it didn't affect me the way I expected it to—and I have become an expert at compartmentalizing my feelings. So when I went to the restaurant, and saw the people who really cared for me, I felt better about myself. The thing with Carlton just happened! You know that I'd never messed around on John before."

"I know," Asia said.

"Now that I think about it, *not* messing around on John was my way of coping with his infidelities; somehow thinking that if I just loved him a little bit more, he wouldn't stray. And he would see me as someone deserving of his love—not just a show piece."

"Well, I'm glad you did it!" Asia said, giving me a hug. "That dirty dog deserved it!"

We laughed together, as Asia wiped away my tears. She handed me a cappuccino.

"You know what was crazy, though?" I said to Asia. "The connection that I made with Carlton is amazing! It was like we knew each other in another life. I can't explain it."

Just then, Lou yelled, "Asia! Someone just pulled up! Are you expecting someone?"

"No!" she yelled outside to Lou. Asia got up. "Now who the hell could this be coming up here?"

Asia walked out to the front porch, and I heard her say, "Oh, shit! It's Carlton! How did he find us?!"

He got out of the car, waved, and said, "Good morning, Asia! I'm looking for Candice."

Just at that moment, I walked out onto on the porch, surprised.

"Carlton! What are you doing here? And how did you find me?" I asked.

"I have to talk to you. Tiny told me you were here. I hope you don't mind, but it's important."

I walked toward him. "Lou, this is my friend Carlton," I said.

"Great meeting you, Lou," Carlton said, shaking Lou's hand. "Great seeing you again, Asia."

"You, too, Carlton," Asia said. She sipped her cappuccino. "Would you like a cup of coffee?" she asked Carlton.

"No, thanks," Carlton said as he looked at me.

"Okay," Asia said. "We'll leave you guys out here to talk."

"What are you doing here?" I asked him again.

Carlton grabbed my hand, and said, "I told you I would find you. I had to talk to you face to face. I know this seems extreme, but Tiny told me it would be okay for me to come up here to see you. Candice," he said. "I can't let you go."